A Song to the Sun

Published in the United States of America

ISBN: 9798645759087

Photo Credits:

www.freepik.com
www.clipart-library.com
www.cliparting.com
www.kindpng.com

First Edition (2020)

Acknowledgments

I'd like to take this opportunity to acknowledge and thank my family for their continuous love, inspiration, and support for all my creative endeavors. Especially to my wonderful wife Deandra, who urges me to focus without fear. She is very much a coach even though she may not know it.

This book is dedicated to the curious child in all of us that smiles on sunny days and loves to go outside and marvel at the beautiful things that nature is and has to offer to all of us that take notice. Most of all this book is dedicated to the universal "People of the Sun"...Shine On.

A Song to the Sun

By **David W. Harris**

Ilustrated By **Laurian Studesville**

I sing a song to the Sun with a voice so big.
I sing a song to the Sun like my ancestors did.

I sing a song to the Sun. I bet it's full of wisdom.

I sing a song to the Sun. It is my friend. It nourishes the soil and it warms my skin.

It sings to the buffaloes.
It sings to the bears.
It sings to the peaches.
It sings to the pears.

It sings back to the plants. It sings to the butterflies; it sings to the ants.

It sings to the farms.
It sings to the city.
It sings to the big things
and things itty-bitty.

It sings back to the bees.
It sings to the rivers and sings to the trees.

I sing a song to the Sun.
Do you know it's a
sphere?

And even though it rains, it will never disappear.

I sing a song to the Sun.
I hope the song makes it glad.
It's the first source of light
That the world ever had.

I sing a song to the Sun. Did you know that it's a star? Sometimes I imagine I can hold it in a jar.

I sing a song to the Sun. In Spanish the word is "sol".

It's the light of the world,
from North to South Pole.

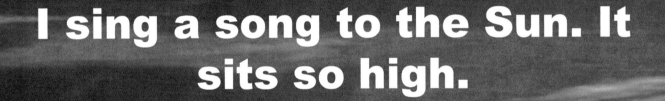

I sing a song to the Sun. It sits so high.

I think it winks at the planes when they fly through the sky.

I sing a song to the Sun in the highest of notes.

I sing a song to the Sun. It shines so bright.

Many times I have tried to touch it with my kite.

I sing a song to the Sun.
It's my fun little game.
It goes to work everyday
and never complains.

And when we don't see it, I guess it needs a break. Then it comes back to shine, no matter how long it takes.

I sing a song to the Sun.
When I dance in the yard.
I sing a song to the Sun.
The words are not hard.

"You light up the world. You light up my life. You light up my soul. We're both full of light."

"You're high in the sky.
You can't be blocked.

*Clouds try it all the time,
but you can't be stopped."*

*"That's my song to the Sun.
You can sing it if you choose.
Sing it on a sunny day
even if you get the blues."*

"That's my song to the Sun.
It's my fancy little thing.
In the Universal kingdom,
the Sun is still King"

Made in the USA
Las Vegas, NV
13 February 2023

67446264R00031